UNDER
a
MANTLE
of
STARS

Manuel Puig

UNDER
a
MANTLE
of
STARS

Revised Edition

Translated by
Ronald Christ

Lumen Books

Lumen Books
446 West 20 Street
New York, N.Y. 10011

Printed in the United States of America.

ISBN: 0-930829-32-8

A Note on the Revised Edition

After its first production, two things troubled Manuel Puig about *Under a Mantle of Stars:* the style of the acting and the ending. Like the characters in the play itself, he cared about *how*, about the *way*, people were; and in his role of play-wright that meant he cared about how the actors were his people on stage. From the first production on, he was dis-tressed. "All they want is to camp," he told me, "or, worse, to really *ACT*." While he thought that camping would be the bad temptation for any U.S. production, he hoped that stage directions would dissuade the actors or at least convey his intention for their style of being on the stage. Therefore, on the basis of his experience with the play in production, we added certain things to the translation that were not in the Spanish. For example, after the Father announces his incur-able illness, like "a bad actor," he is to limp, stiff-legged. Puig wanted to spoil the performer's chance for a grand scene, and his preemptive measure perhaps lets you see why he believed that the only right production, naturally theatri-cal, would be Italian.

The problem of the acting can only be solved, really, in rehearsal and performance; Puig alone could resolve the problem of the ending. When we reviewed the translation, we talked a lot about the end and considered several solu-tions. Nothing different quite satisfied him. Yet he was right to ponder it, as later criticism by Gabriela Mora showed, among other things (*Dispositio* 13, 1988); I think he never read her article, but he knew its argument. A year or so be-fore his death, Puig drafted a new ending—more accurately, an addition to the old—and I translated it. Until now, it lay in my files.

This new ending emphatically stops the play from ending. Where it formerly closed with a ringing doorbell that implied still another repetition of the action—one more variation on that theme of the Eternal Return practiced by contemporary Latin American writers—the new ending makes the dream's continuance explicit. The characters dream on under their waking mantle of stars, a recurring dream that is also never-ending. What's more, the new ending explicitly proclaims the symbolism of identity and order the play so pleasure-takingly develops. (Puig also replaced one other line in the text—one of the most disputed during our talks—so as to manifest his theme of language; rather, his theme of the non-verbal.).

Puig was no tinkerer. He worked diligently and revised relentlessly, seeking in his plays the *shorter* and the *better*. (Believing that the latter often resulted from the former.) In the issue of *World Literature Today* dedicated to "The Posthumous Career of Manuel Puig" (Autumn, 1991). I wrote that we read the translation to each other over and over, switching parts, discussing everything. (He read it with others, too, and hefted each suggestion.) We never got to test the new ending that way, only by exchange of drafts, which he approved; yet, his last revisions, so satisfying, fulfill much that we talked about. This revised ending carries through another gesture into his posthumous career.

Myself, I would prefer yet another revision. In mine, the phone rings and Manuel—speaking in syllables more than whole words, teasing each one in two-note flamenco—tells me when we're meeting to continue working on the untitled drama he left before escaping from under this mantle of stars. The telephone Manuel was quintessential. In literature and life, he gave overheard voices to others (and to himself), and he invented the device of the phone conversation where the un-overheard party sounds clear. He occupies one of those eloquent ellipses now . . . I would tell him the connection's good.

R.C.
1992

Act I

Setting: a spacious living room in an elegant country house. The decor is post-art nouveau and pre-art deco. The year is 1948. It is afternoon and the sunlight has not yet begun to fade. The masters of the house are found seated in the room. Their age is indeterminate: one might guess them to be in their fifties. They also are elegant, but in a very sober, opaque fashion, almost as if they were visible through a grey veil. It is especially striking that the woman has grey hair. Their clothes correspond to the prevailing stereotype of the rural bourgeosie. He is reading the newspaper; she is doing needlework. Nothing is realistic, everything stylized, including the characters' speech.

MASTER
(Suddenly dropping the newspaper at his side, annoyed) I can't even read the paper! It's useless trying to distract myself. I can't get the idea out of my head.

MISTRESS
(Conciliatory, but not especially patient) I'm sure she's coming back. She'll be here before it gets dark.

MASTER
(Gets up, paces nervously) If only she were our daughter, then we could try to understand her. By way of our own quirks, I mean.

MISTRESS
We *did* raise her.

MASTER
Tonight, darkness is going to swallow her up.

MISTRESS
And some bright, sunny morning we're going to understand her.

MASTER
But she's got other blood, other shadows in her veins. And

you can hardly remember the parents, just the way they were, any more than I can. Over the years, we've changed that last image according to our whims. You have embroidered a fleur-de-lis on his chest, just like one of your tapestries.

MISTRESS
Almost twenty years have gone by, and there is something to what you say. We can't possibly remember them as they were.

MASTER
Him—oh, I certainly remember. I see him brought back to life in certain lunatic things his daughter does.

MISTRESS
But it's unfair—to the girl—associating her with that day in the life of her father, his last day. Weren't you two inseparable friends all through your early life? Was one outburst from that . . . insignificant wife enough to destroy your friendship with him?

MASTER
(Disheartened) I wouldn't want anybody to be in my position.

MISTRESS
Oh, why be so negative? . . . With or without problems, the girl is ours now. What would have become of us without her? She has filled our days. Just think if she hadn't been born before the accident. You'd still be in the same rage, still have the same doubts. That imbecile wife's phone call, accusing me of adultery, would still be ringing in your ears.

MASTER
They left the child with somebody or other, got into the car with the top down and drove off. They took the curves too fast. He really was my friend, and he was coming here to rid me of that doubt, to tell me it was all a misunderstanding—or was he coming to take my wife away?

2

MISTRESS

If he was coming to take me away, he would've taken the curves more carefully. My God! . . . how boring, answering the same questions over and over for twenty years! That's why I like listening to serials on the radio.

MASTER

Just like a housemaid.

MISTRESS

Don't speak of the devil. Are you sure you put up the ad in a good spot?

MASTER

Yes, I left it in the agency window, and they promised that today they would send that young girl . . .

MISTRESS

(Finishes his sentence) . . . that young girl who will be just as perfect—let's hope!—as they described her to you! *(Raises her face, for the first time, from her needlework)* Such a tragic face!

MASTER

Without servants there is no time for tragedy, only a sordid bourgeois drama. Passion burns out while you're washing your own dishes and emptying the ashtrays.

MISTRESS

It's better that way . . . tragedies on the radio, with background music by the great masters. *(Her expression clouds over, her ironic tone vanishes.)* It's this golden sunlight, at four in the afternoon, that stops us from forgetting. We were right here, waiting.

MASTER

The car crashed, and they died instantly—just a few minutes from our door.

MISTRESS

(Regains her usual self-control) But they left us with the

3

very best of themselves—the daughter. Who is neither strange nor insane. She is . . . simply herself. Incomprehensible, period. Like everyone else.

MASTER
But why disappear like this, for hours and hours? She gets up on her horse, and all the horizon shows, far as the eye can see, is some lonesome tree.

MISTRESS
Does it really bother you so much?

MASTER
It's just that one begins to realize . . . *(He does not dare to finish.)*

MISTRESS
(Beginning to share her husband's concern) What?

MASTER
That she's *so* miserable.

MISTRESS
It's not just the usual ups and downs of a girl her age?

MASTER
But what if someday we find out, and it's too late? If one day she can't stand the suffering any more, and she does something foolish? . . . I'm very uneasy about this. *(He goes to the telephone.)*

MISTRESS
What are you doing?

MASTER
(To the operator) The psychiatric hospital in town, please.

MISTRESS
But what if she finds out? Don't give them her name!

MASTER
(Into the telephone, uneasily) Excuse me . . . Just for infor-

mation . . . In case of an emergency, just in case somebody might need help . . . Here, only a few miles . . . but out in the middle of the country . . . The name? Whose name? . . . No . . . The patient? . . . No . . . I'm not . . . I am . . . the man of the house . . . My name? Why? Yes, the emergency might be . . . serious . . . No, the name, no . . . *(Hangs up abruptly)*

MISTRESS
Now they're going to suspect . . . They can trace our number through the operator.

MASTER
It doesn't matter.

MISTRESS
Care to tell me what you've gained with that absurd call? *(The doorbell rings.)* Who can that be?

MASTER
The maid, thank the Lord.

MISTRESS
(She goes to open the front door.) We're saved.

DAUGHTER
(The fresh voice of a young girl, full of life, radiant, speaking from outside) Mama, it's me!

MISTRESS
(Opens the door) Oh . . . it's you!

DAUGHTER
(Dressed according to the dictates of the 1948 Dior "New Look," she is attractive though somewhat ingenuous.) Some disappointment, isn't it?

MASTER
(Irritated) May one know what you've been up to? *(Resumes staring at the newspaper, pretending not to be interested in the girl)*

5

DAUGHTER
(To the Mistress) I left without my key. I forgot to take it.

MASTER
What were you thinking of?

DAUGHTER
I forgot it, just the way I sometimes forget what I want out of life.

MASTER
(Without lifting his head from the paper) What is it you want?

MISTRESS
Enough of these profundities! She forgets her little whims, that's all she forgets!

DAUGHTER
No, I really do forget what I want most out of life.

MASTER
(Folds the newspaper, throws his head back, leaning it on the back of the sofa, signaling his deep concern) This morning I had promised myself to work the whole day. You know perfectly well the enormous job ahead of me: to recall the memories of an entire lifetime.

DAUGHTER
Papa, I'm sorry if I upset you . . .

MASTER
Just waking up and not finding you was enough.

DAUGHTER
I had to get out in the open, that's all.

MISTRESS
But I noticed you hadn't taken your purse with the money in it. What did you do for lunch?

DAUGHTER
I grabbed some fruit. There's plenty around. Before I forget, he's not coming tonight . . . my fiancé, I mean. He says hello to you both. He called this morning.

MISTRESS
You know I adore him, but tonight, I'd really prefer listening to the latest episode of the serial. *(Addresses her husband)* And you?

MASTER
I don't adore him, and, oddly enough, I too would prefer listening to the serial. *(He becomes serious.)* And so this is what two women have turned me into: *(To the Daughter)* an alarmist father *(To the Mistress)* and a radio listener.

MISTRESS
Last night, on account of arguing with your father, I missed the episode.

DAUGHTER
I heard it.

MISTRESS
Tell me what happened, right now.

DAUGHTER
Later . . . *(To the Master)* Papa, every single minute of yours is precious. For my sake, please, take advantage of the few remaining hours this afternoon.

MASTER
(With an obvious weakness for the Daughter) Thank you. I'll do what I can. *(Exits, but exchanges an enigmatic look with the Mistress just before leaving)*

DAUGHTER
(Softly, so her father cannot hear) Something terrible's happened, but you have to promise me you won't say a word to him. *(Points stage left, where the Master exited)*

MISTRESS
Of course not . . .

DAUGHTER
Antonio's not coming tonight—or ever again. He's going to marry another woman. Just as I predicted, he's deserted me.

MISTRESS
But why?

DAUGHTER
There's only one possible reason: *(Breathes in deeply, resentful)* marrying for money. She is very rich. But don't say a word to him *(Points again to where the Master exited)* or he'll make a scene.

MISTRESS
Hadn't you noticed anything?

DAUGHTER
From the very start I had the feeling that something bad was going to happen. The joy he brought me was too great, and on my own I began imagining difficulties. From that point to their coming about was a short step.

MISTRESS
Don't beat around the bush. Tell me the facts.

DAUGHTER
I'm sorry, but if you don't listen to me, you're never going to understand. He gave meaning to my life.

MISTRESS
Oh, surely that's not true. You were a happy girl before him.

DAUGHTER
He arrived at the dance that night with another woman. It was the first time I ever saw him, but I had the definite feeling he was someone I'd found before—and lost. And

8

that's what had always disturbed my life, like the moon churning the tides of the sea.

MISTRESS
(Downplaying the significance of what the Daughter has just said) I was eighteen once, too, with an idle imagination.

DAUGHTER
Suddenly all the other men at the dance seemed dull and empty. I took refuge in the library of that big old house, in the dark. My anguish seemed to subside.

MISTRESS
(Ironically) Suddenly you heard someone breathing.

DAUGHTER
(Challengingly) Yes. And his voice. He asked me something. He asked me to describe what he was like, but without seeing him, in the dark. "Why?" I asked.

MISTRESS
(Even more ironically) Couldn't he recognize himself?

DAUGHTER
He answered that he was lost, and I should point out what he had to do. I shut my eyes in the darkness, and I saw a lake of clear blue liquid that I'd always wished for . . . to drink? . . . to float on? A brilliant blue, with even brighter trimmings. Or did I see some precious stone? An enormous aquamarine, with me swimming inside it. And then he, the one who was lost, changed the tone of his voice, suddenly seeming pleased, and he told me to follow him, because there was still another, an even better place, and I couldn't imagine it for myself. I had seen the entire world, and it was this precious stone, but he told me I was forgetting something: the landscapes inside me, the mountains dark with hatred, the jungles of suffering, where rays of light, like doubts, filtered in, and once again the lake. Only now it is inside me, and someone else must submerge himself in me to appreciate the freshness of the water.

MISTRESS
(Ironically) A man showed me visions once, too. But I've forgotten them now.

DAUGHTER
I don't ever want to forget them!

MISTRESS
But time takes over, and puts an end to both the good and the bad memories—as well as the desire to live.

DAUGHTER
You really don't remember what you felt?

MISTRESS
No, I've forgotten everything.

DAUGHTER
Antonio will never come here again, but *(Gestures stage left)* nobody here should find out. *(An automobile is heard approaching.)*

MISTRESS
Somebody's coming . . .

DAUGHTER
Who could it be? . . .

MASTER
(Appears at the head of the stairs) Are you expecting anybody? From the window I saw a convertible driving up.

MISTRESS
Let's hope it's the maid.

MASTER
(Coming down the stairs) In a convertible? *(He asks for silence with a gesture; the car is heard to stop; two car doors open and close, followed by the sound of the front doorbell.)* I'll get it. *(He opens the door. A very elegant couple stands in the shadow of the doorway. They are*

dressed in the fashion of 1929, almost in full dress you would say. They are young, in their early thirties; but, at the same time, their worldly air makes them seem older, of an indeterminate age.) Hello. What can I do for you?

VISITOR
(Very self-possessed but cordial and polite) Excuse the intrusion, sir, but . . .

LADY VISITOR
(She finishes his sentence) . . . we were on our way to a place not far from here, and we ran out of gas.

VISITOR
We really have a little left, but we were afraid of ending up in the middle of the countryside, so we stopped here. Are you the man of the house?

MASTER
(Very surprised at recognizing the Visitors when he steps closer to them) Yes, I am, and it's no intrusion. We'll send for some gasoline . . .

MISTRESS
(She reacts as he did, but with control, finishing his sentence.) . . . as soon as the maid gets here, which can't be very long now. But do come in, please. Don't stand out there.

VISITOR
Thank you, madam.

LADY VISITOR
What an inviting room! But don't I recognize it from somewhere? Could it possibly have appeared as a model in one of those interior decorating magazines?

DAUGHTER
Our visitors are going to a masked ball. But are you going to wear masks?

MISTRESS
My dear, don't question people so.

MASTER
Such beautiful clothes, those of twenty years ago.

VISITOR
Excuse me, but I owe a reply to the young lady. Yes, we're going to wear masks.

DAUGHTER
Who do you want to pass for?

VISITOR
For two terrible jewel thieves.

MISTRESS
Do sit down, please.

MASTER
Have you driven far?

LADY VISITOR
Now it's me who's owed a reply. Where can I have seen this charming decor?

DAUGHTER
It's not original. We copied it out of one of the foreign magazines.

MASTER
But you must be thirsty. Driving always parches the throat.

VISITOR
For me, fresh water from that well I saw when we drove up.

MISTRESS
All right. *(To the Master)* Please, you get the water, and *(To the Daughter)* you get the teapot ready. *(To the Visitors)* Excuse me for a moment, while I get the teacups.

DAUGHTER
(To the Visitors) Excuse me, please. *(Exits)*

MASTER
Excuse me. *(Exits)*

MISTRESS
(Alone with the Visitors) The two of you . . . how can it be?

VISITOR
Do you know us from somewhere?

LADY VISITOR
Yes, she's recognized us . . . *(Approaches the Mistress, perhaps pretending to recognize her)* in spite of our disguise . . .

MISTRESS
On the contrary. Except for those clothes, it might never have entered my mind that it was you.

DAUGHTER
(Appears at the extreme left, downstage) What kind of tea would you like?

LADY VISITOR
Whichever you prefer. I want to have my tea with you.

MISTRESS
(To the Daughter) I'll help you and *(To the Visitor)* be back in just one minute. *(Exits, taking the Daughter with her)*

LADY VISITOR
(Alone with her partner) How stupid to mention the jewels!

VISITOR
(Humorously) Whoever's going to imagine that two people on their way to a masked ball are hiding such a cargo?

LADY VISITOR
(Very disturbed) Are you sure no one followed us?

VISITOR
Sure. But the ones I don't trust are these people. Where should we hide . . . the loot?

LADY VISITOR
It's not loot. It belongs to us, and if you don't feel that it's yours, well, that's your problem, and the stuff's mine then. *(Finishing the sentence, she contradictorily hands him a silk bag filled with jewels.)*

VISITOR
(Looks around the room) Where should I put it?

LADY VISITOR
(Lifting up a cushion from the sofa) No one will suspect this fluffy cushion. *(He puts the bag under the cushion.)* But don't talk to me about anything fluffy. I'm tired to death.

VISITOR
(Ironically) Well, you like the house. Maybe you'd like to stay here . . .

LADY VISITOR
Yes, I like it, in spite of these bumpkins.

VISITOR
I could leave you here, if you'd prefer it that way.

LADY VISITOR
If you dare leave me, the bosses will turn against you.

VISITOR
(Defiantly) I'm not so sure about that.

LADY VISITOR
I only have to say one word.

VISITOR
You wouldn't dare!

14

LADY VISITOR
Just one word from me will destroy you.

VISITOR
They're coming . . .

MASTER
(Enters with a cut-glass goblet and an expensive crystal pitcher on a silver tray) Fresh water from the well. *(Looks behind him)* The girl's making the tea, she can't hear us . . .

LADY VISITOR
(Ambiguously) Has our arrival caused you a great bother?

MASTER
(Annoyed) Let's not talk in circles while she's out of the room . . . *(Moves to the Lady Visitor and hugs her like an old, much-loved friend)* The two of you! *(With real emotion)* It just can't be . . . You could be an halluciantion . . .

VISITOR
Well, perhaps we are one . . .

MASTER
Seems like not a single day has gone by. She . . . is your daughter.

LADY VISITOR
(Entering into the game) She doesn't know we're alive then.

MASTER
She believes you both died in the accident, and we told her that we're her foster parents.

LADY VISITOR
What shall we do? Reveal ourselves?

VISITOR
Not right away. That might cause an emotional shock.

MASTER
Let her react on her own. Maybe she'll recognize you naturally. Blood is thicker than water.

DAUGHTER
(She suddenly appears with the tea tray, completely preoccupied with it. The Mistress follows.) This is a kind of tea that has to steep for a few minutes. I hope you like it. Anyway, it's my favorite, as you requested.

LADY VISITOR
Thank you.

MISTRESS
But, please, won't you sit down?

MASTER
(Very confused) I'm sorry I didn't offer earlier.

VISITOR
(Going to sit down) Your cushions look really soft and fluffy.

LADY VISITOR
(Seating herself on the cushion covering the jewels) They are.

MASTER
(Finally offering the water) Your water. *(The Daughter snatches the goblet and serves him.)*

VISITOR
Really, the idea fascinates me: drinking rain water. It's almost like sharing in the freshness of the countryside.

LADY VISITOR
(With an air of jealousy to her irony) And the freshness of youth. While I feel like a ship's figurehead next to these women, so natural, wearing no cosmetics.

DAUGHTER

(Rapturously) Oh, but we both want to be you. Because you've achieved everything you set out to do. You love this man and he is . . . *(Caught between her fascination with the Lady Visitor's powerful aura and a feeling of indignation, as yet unclarified)* bound to you, maybe forever. Out of everything in the world, he responded to your call.

MISTRESS

Excuse her, please. She gets carried away.

VISITOR

I find her charming. She dares to say whatever comes into her mind.

MASTER

Which is one form of madness. *(To the Daughter)* That's enough, please!

DAUGHTER

(To the Lady Visitor) I always wanted to be you, just as if you were someone I'd known before. But the problem for me is, there can't be two people just the same. *(Pointing to the Lady Visitor)* When you walked through that door, I knew who the conqueror was . . .

LADY VISITOR

(Deeply moved by something still unclear) As if you'd known me before . . . You did say that, didn't you?

DAUGHTER

Yes, as if I had seen you somewhere else. Or as if I'd heard a lot about you. Yes, that's it. And then I would have pictured you exactly as I pleased. Less powerful, maybe. But you appear here, and then there's nothing else for me to do but admit it. The conqueror is . . . *(Points to the Lady Visitor again)*

LADY VISITOR

(Deeply affected) I would like to be exactly the way you

pictured me . . . *(Smiling)* less fearsome, less powerful, more lovable, right?

MASTER
A child's foolishness! You're splendid just the way you are.

LADY VISITOR
I feel so weary . . . all of a sudden.

MISTRESS
The tea might revive you. You haven't even wet your lips.

LADY VISITOR
Would it be possible . . . for me to lie down, just for a little while?

DAUGHTER
Yes, of course. *(Looks at the Master)* Let's take her up to my room. It's quiet enough there, don't you think?

MASTER
Yes. *(Stands up)* Here, lean on my arm.

LADY VISITOR
Thank you. *(To the Visitor)* Can you do without me for a moment?

VISITOR
Please . . .

MASTER
Rest yourself a bit. Just think, a grand ball lies ahead of you, isn't that so?

VISITOR
(To the Lady Visitor) Don't worry about me. *(To the others)* Meanwhile, I'd like to venture out into the garden. I caught a glimpse of a strange, though delicate efflorescence, just at the point of opening up.

MISTRESS
(To the Daughter) Take good care of the lady.

DAUGHTER
Don't worry.

MASTER
(He leads the Lady Visitor and the Daughter up the stairs and speaks to his wife with evident irony.) And you take care of the gentleman.

MISTRESS
For the moment, I propose that we all gather down here at eight o'clock for a glass of champagne.

MASTER
For the moment, make certain he helps himself to whatever he wants. *(They go up the stairs.)*

VISITOR
Your husband is very kind.

MISTRESS
Do you really want to go out into the garden? *(She walks about the room to make sure that no one can see her from upstairs.)* You've finally come . . . you kept your word.

VISITOR
(Unsure how to react) They can hear you . . . *(Gets up)*

MISTRESS
If you love me as much as I love you, you must realize that hope never dies. When there's so much love, there's no resigning yourself to losing the other. Deep down inside, something kept telling me I'd see you again, even in this world.

VISITOR
(Stalling) Is that so? . . .

MISTRESS

Is it possible the waiting is over? You can't imagine. These
have been years of taking care of myself, of exercise, diet-
ing, massages. Everything, so you would find me fit. To
wait, always to wait . . . in this world. Now my greatest
fear is that hell might be just that: to wait for you eternally,
without your ever arriving.

VISITOR

(Entering into the game) Fear neither hell, nor anything else
. . . because I am here.

MISTRESS

What helped me through each day was . . . your daughter. I
always thought I could catch some trait of yours in her: her
way of laying her head on the pillow, of rubbing her hands
together when it grew cold.

VISITOR

(Even more ambiguously) She's a lovely girl. I'm charmed
by her.

MISTRESS

Just today we were talking, and she frightened me: repeat-
ing things I'd told her, as if they'd happened to her. Besides
. . . they were things you had said to me. Things you remember, maybe. Very precise words.

VISITOR

A lot of years have gone by . . .

MISTRESS

You spoke them to me, one afternoon. I nestled in your
arms, the sun was beginning to set, just like this very moment. This time of day always frightens me, the death of the
day. Because it's not absolutely certain the sun will always
rise again. One day or another, things die. That afternoon
when I was waiting for you . . . with him, waiting for you
and for . . . that woman, it was growing dark . . . and for
me the dawn never came again. Even now, as I'm looking
at you, everything is still plunged in deepest darkness . . .

VISITOR
But I'm here . . .

MISTRESS
I can't convince myself. You're a phantom. My lips remain
frozen . . . like my thighs.

VISITOR
I'm no phantom. I'm an ordinary man. In a few hours you'll
be able to see my beard growing.

MISTRESS
If you could recall those words, I'd really believe that you
are here—in the flesh.

VISITOR
It's a long time ago, you'll have to give me some help. At
least give me a hint how to start.

MISTRESS
The start . . . from the start I had the feeling that something
bad was going to happen. The joy you brought me was too
great, and on my own I began imagining difficulties. From
that point to their coming about was a short step.

VISITOR
(Feeling his way, not knowing what to say) You should have
thought about me, about what . . . I'd suffer.

MISTRESS
You arrived at the dance that night with another woman. It
was the first time I ever saw you, but I had the definite
feeling you were someone I'd found before—and lost.

VISITOR
(Trying to lighten the tone a bit) But what about the other
men at the dance, didn't they prevent you from getting to
me?

MISTRESS
I took refuge in the library of that big old house, in the dark.

21

VISITOR
How could I find you in the dark?

MISTRESS
I heard you breathing.

VISITOR
(Trying to follow her lead) Of course. I was someone you'd found before—and lost.

MISTRESS
(Fascinated) Lost! I see you're beginning to recall. Because that's the very first word you uttered in that darkened library: "Lost. I'm lost." And you asked me to describe, without opening my eyes, how you were.

VISITOR
What did you answer me?

MISTRESS
You have to recall. Try hard.

VISITOR
(Not knowing what to say) I've already recalled one thing.

MISTRESS
Yes, that's right. I'll help you a little more. I answered you, without opening my eyes, that I saw a lake, bright blue. Or was it a precious stone? And then you told me to follow, because there was another place, even better, only I couldn't imagine it by myself.

VISITOR
Go on.

MISRESS
Let's see . . . what was that other place?

VISITOR
Go on, a little more.

MISTRESS

No. Now it's your turn to go on with the story.

VISITOR

This is *your* story. Maybe I have a different one to tell you.

MISTRESS

No. I don't want to hear anything but our story. I don't want to know about anything that might separate us, only about what unites us.

VISITOR

But what about my feelings? You're not interested in knowing about them? Right now I may be going through a terrible crisis. I may need help. Because . . . the truth—for this once—may have escaped your imagination.

MISTRESS

(Playfully) You're testing me, with fibs. I know you're strong, and there's never any need to worry about you. You're not going to fool me. I remember you just the way you were. Strong.

VISITOR

Just the way I still am . . . strong.

MISTRESS

But I want you to repeat the rest, without any help from me . . . later. You'll have to tell me what that other place was, where you led me. Now, it's almost night, I want to appear before you . . . later, in full regalia . . . I'll leave you here for quite a while . . . . I want to adorn myself . . . I want you to see me at my very best . . . Because now the waiting is over. Tonight I want to blaze, to consume myself in the flame of pleasure, even if it's only once more in my existence . . . I want to feel alive. Like those times I used to fall into your arms, on those afternoons in 1929. They were very long, those afternoons.

VISITOR

Don't take too long . . .

23

MISTRESS

(Ironically) I'm going to, but you will wait for me. Now it's your turn. *(She disappears up the stairs. The Visitor remains perplexed, but at the same time amused. He stretches out on the sofa, worn out after so much feminine effusiveness, and seems to rest. The Daughter comes down the stairs. Seeing him apparently asleep, she approaches on tiptoe, strokes his forehead devotedly. He jumps up, but doesn't succeed in standing, because she has sat down next to him and taken hold of his wrists.)*

DAUGHTER

I've got you at my mercy . . .

VISITOR

(He does not know how to react; he obviously does not know her.) No doubt about that.

DAUGHTER

What a crazy idea of yours! Showing up in disguise. *(She strokes his chest and stands up.)*

VISITOR

(Taking the opportunity to stand up too) You . . .

DAUGHTER

I took you by surprise? *(She can no longer restrain her desire to embrace him and throws herself into his arms.)* Antonio! Your call this morning almost cost me my life. But now you're here, and it doesn't matter that you've brought her. What's important is holding you in my arms.

VISITOR

It doesn't matter to you . . . about her?

DAUGHTER

(Breaks out of the embrace) I hate her! And I also hate that fake beard. *(Tears away his artificial beard)*

VISITOR

My companion is dangerous. She must not find out . . . about us.

DAUGHTER
Then she doesn't know . . . that we were engaged, until only a few hours ago, this very morning?

VISITOR
If she finds out, your life—or mine—will be in danger. We have to pretend you've just met me.

DAUGHTER
The truth is, I don't know you. We never made love. Remember, I'm a modern woman, and this is 1948, not the 1920s of your disguise. I'm emancipated. I smoke. And I drink cocktails. And just because I let you put your hands all over my body doesn't mean you know me either. I'm modern, and I know that we will only know each other on the day our flesh is one.

VISITOR
(Aroused) I've put my hands all over your body, but what about yours all over mine?

DAUGHTER
I said I was modern, not libertine.

VISITOR
Touch me.

DAUGHTER
What are you saying?

VISITOR
Touch me.

DAUGHTER
Why? To give you a cheap thrill?

VISITOR
(He is caught up by his strong desire for the young girl and, at the same time, spurred on by the ambiguity of the situation.) It's just that I'm lost. I've lost myself. And if your hands find me, they'll know how to lead me where I ought to be.

DAUGHTER
(Deeply fascinated) Lost?

VISITOR
I beg you to tell me, without opening your eyes, how I am.

DAUGHTER
(Taken in by the Visitor's ruse) Without opening my eyes, I see only the dark landscapes inside me. I'm searching for a place, which they say is inside me, but I don't find it. Someone else has to submerge himself, in my mind, to appreciate the freshness . . . of the water.

VISITOR
A bright-colored lake.

DAUGHTER
(Gratefully surprised) How do you know that?

VISITOR
You didn't remember?

DAUGHTER
No . . . As soon as you came through that door, I forgot a lot of things. Whatever was beautiful to me before stopped being beautiful, unless it's linked to you somehow.

VISITOR
Could this be the first time you're seeing me?

DAUGHTER
In a certain way, yes.

VISITOR
I peer down into the lake so I can see myself reflected in those brilliant blue waters. Or is it some precious stone?

DAUGHTER
(Lighting up) Your voice is changing. Suddenly you seem pleased.

VISITOR
Because, in a few moments, I'm going to know you. *(Begins to undress her)* But I still can't see myself reflected in the water, such as I am.

DAUGHTER
Maybe that's because inside me the mountains still lie deep in the darkness of night.

VISITOR
It's because you've hidden yourself away in the library of that big old house, in the dark. We'll get out of there.

DAUGHTER
(Dazed by the coincidence of the images) Oh! . . . I don't know how to get out of there.

VISITOR
Touch me. That's all it takes.

DAUGHTER
(After delicately kissing him) You asked me to describe how you are?

VISITOR
(Now really in need of help) Yes, tell me please.

DAUGHTER
You are exactly as I had always imagined you—the man of my dreams.

VISITOR
No, I, I myself, how am I? . . . I may be in some danger, under the power of some ruthless person, threatened by some crime syndicate. I need your help.

DAUGHTER
You are exactly the one I desired.

VISITOR
No. The man of your dreams, no. I, I myself, how am I? I

need you to tell me, so I can know what to do. I'm not someone invented by you.

DAUGHTER
I don't understand you. There's only one man in this room, right?

VISITOR
Yes.

DAUGHTER
And it's you.

VISITOR
(Now without the strength to establish the reality) Touch me then. *(He slips his hand under her skirt, then withdraws it, holding her panties.)* As I touch you.

DAUGHTER
I'm afraid I'll fumble with the stubborn knot in your neck-tie, or with a tight buttonhole, and destroy the magic of this moment.

VISITOR
(Bares his chest, suddenly and determinedly) I know my knots and my buttonholes.

DAUGHTER
She's tired, your . . . companion, and she won't come in. But the masters of this house, my dear foster parents, aren't you afraid they'll suddenly appear?

VISITOR
We two are the only ones here.

DAUGHTER
I'm a virgin. I may cry out in pain and spoil everything.

VISITOR
I'll smother any cries with my hand. See? It's a big hand. *(Takes her hand)* My knuckles are twice the size of yours—

to make you knuckle under. *(Begins to undress her; she pulls back. He gags her with his hand. The Lady Visitor appears at the head of the stairs, dressed in a lavish Chinese robe. She is horrified by what she sees and disappears, only to reappear a moment later followed by the Master and Mistress, the latter dressed in a bathrobe and shower-cap. The Visitor goes on undressing the Daughter, who does not resist him. The Masters are also horrified at seeing what is happening, but come down the stairs in silence, following the Lady Visitor.)*

MISTRESS
(On reaching the foot of the stairs, she can no longer control her horror.) Ahhh!

DAUGHTER
(The pair stop when they hear the exclamation and discover three others in the room, a few feet away from their partially uncovered bodies.) Antonio!

VISITOR
Don't move.

MASTER
(Pityingly, always acting on the basis of what, for him, is the delicate mental stability of the Daughter) Don't get upset . . . *(Powerfully restraining the Lady Visitor from attacking the couple)* Whenever a maiden is deflowered, the same thing always happens: she imagines that her parents discover her in the act.

DAUGHTER
No, you are seeing . . .

MASTER
Nothing of the kind. We are an hallucination. It's your guilty conscience that makes you see visions . . . *(He repeats his impressive sign to the Lady Visitor, so that she will join in the farce.)*

LADY VISITOR
(Wickedly) . . . and makes you miss out on the festivities.

MISTRESS
No. How horrible . . . *(The Master silences her by covering her mouth with his hand.)*

LADY VISITOR
Take advantage of this moment, and savor it. Don't be foolish. Leave the sorrow until later. It will come, in ways you know nothing about.

DAUGHTER
(Completely confused) I shouldn't be foolish?

VISITOR
(Resumes undressing her) Or talkative either. *(Led by the Master, the two other women draw back and begin to climb the stairs.)* It's better in silence.

DAUGHTER
(Gives him her full attention again) Why?

VISITOR
Because after a while words may turn against us, caresses never.

DAUGHTER
In silence . . . Oh! . . . Ay! *(He covers her mouth again.)*

VISITOR
Yes, in silence . . . I don't want you talking to the man of your dreams. He may not be here.

CURTAIN

ACT II

Setting: The same as Act I, but in the dark of night. Only one light is on, at stage left, under the staircase. The Master smokes and paces agitatedly, like a moth around a flame. The extreme right of the stage, including the sofa where the couple made love, is in total darkness.

LADY VISITOR
(She is stretched out on the sofa and suddenly an unnatural light falls on her. Until now the audience has not seen her. She is still dressed in the Chinese robe from the previous act, and she holds an unlit cigarette in her mouth.) Do you have a light?

MASTER
(Very surprised) What! You frightened me.

LADY VISITOR
I've been watching you for quite some time.

MASTER
(Approaching to light her cigarette) I didn't see you.

LADY VISITOR
There's no one blinder than he who doesn't want to see.

MASTER
It's because I'm very nervous, and very confused.

LADY VISITOR
I'm melancholy, which is worse.

MASTER
No. The worst thing is worrying about a loved one. That girl is all we have in life.

LADY VISITOR
Look, everything's not lost. What we've got to do is act, but quickly. And not let our lives be governed by irresponsible types, no matter how much we love them. To love is

one thing; to let yourself be manipulated is another.

MASTER
I don't have the slightest idea of what to do. With things as they are, I'm terrified to take even one step. That little girl's psyche is very fragile. She can be hurt very easily.

LADY VISITOR
Calm down, she is not the . . . the little girl you think. She knows perfectly well what she wants, and she doesn't care who she snatches it from.

MASTER
She's not aware of what she's doing.

LADY VISITOR
She has no scruples, which is something else altogether. What she doesn't know is the kind of louse she's gotten herself mixed up with.

MASTER
If he's a louse, why are you with him?

LADY VISITOR
In this case, the danger lies in not knowing who he is. Once you know that, and treat him accordingly, everything untangles itself perfectly.

MASTER
You say it's necessary to act. But how?

LADY VISITOR
The first step is to realize there's a plot to eliminate us. You and me. Later, there will be a third victim, eventually a fourth, and finally, of course, a single survivor.

MASTER
Why plot against me?

LADY VISITOR
You maintain order, and somebody doesn't find that convenient.

MASTER
But why against you?

LADY VISITOR
No one can love me.

MASTER
What are you saying? You're beautiful!

LADY VISITOR
I have power.

MASTER
What power?

LADY VISITOR
It's beside the point to specify. Power such as money gives you, for example. Everyone envies my power. I could destroy him, whenever I like. He knows it and fears me. That's why he can't love me. Power is a curse.

MASTER
No, being powerless is. When I think that one day I may die, leaving that child defenseless, I'm shattered by torment.

LADY VISITOR
No doubt about it: you are mortal. And worse still, three people want you dead. *(A clock strikes.)*

MASTER
Eight o'clock. They'll be coming down now.

LADY VISITOR
I've got an idea. You have to tell a lie . . . *(The Mistress is heard coming down the stairs; she is elegantly attired.)* Come over here with me. *(She leads him stage right, where there is no light. They talk. Meanwhile, the Mistress reaches the bottom of the stairs and takes glasses out of the cabinet for the champagne.)*

MASTER
I know what lie I have to tell . . .

LADY VISITOR
A lie that smashes all their plans into the ground.

MASTER
I'm going to make them tremble . . . to cry with regret.

VISITOR
(He enters from the garden. He is wearing the false beard and has put his shirt on again, but his sleeves are rolled up and his collar is unbuttoned. He speaks to the Lady Visitor and the Master.) Plotting in the dark?

MISTRESS
Ahh! . . . I was asking myself where all of you could be.

VISITOR
I'm always on time. I was invited for a glass of champagne, and here I am.

MASTER
(To the Visitor) Did you see the garden?

VISITOR
An orgy of fragrances! The night is pitch black, and I couldn't make out the colors, but the perfumes seemed stronger every minute. They were seducing me, making themselves indispensable. I'll never be able to forget that garden, I'll always miss that perfume . . . go wherever I go, *(Looks at the Lady Visitor)* be with whomever I'll be with . . .

LADY VISITOR
A good cold in the head, and it will all vanish . . .

MASTER
(With veiled maliciousness) I was worried, thinking you might be bored, all alone, with nothing to do, while the lady rested. But *I* had something to do. You see, I'm writing my memoirs.

34

DAUGHTER
(Coming down the stairs, very well dressed, all in white, luminous, springlike) But don't you think you're very young to be writing your memoirs?

MISTRESS
We're all here now, so let's make a toast, because I'm thirsty. *(She begins to pour the champagne.)*

DAUGHTER
What are we toasting? It's so important to choose the words precisely.

LADY VISITOR
Precisely?

DAUGHTER
Yes, I feel . . . happy, and I'd like everybody to share my feelings. I'd like to find the word that will have this same effect on everybody here.

LADY VISITOR
This effect you're talking about—it lasts about half an hour . . . and afterwards, best go to sleep. Because while it seems this happiness is forever, any mishap can break the spell. The spell of the champagne, of course. That's what I'm talking about.

MISTRESS
(Deeply involved) Better not try to find that word, then.

VISITOR
I'll propose one.

MASTER
Which? I have one to propose as well.

VISITOR
I want to drink a toast to . . . Antonio. This young lady is in love with a young man named Antonio, who makes her happy. In turn, the daughter's happiness makes her parents

happy, so they open their doors to share it all with the rest of the world—in this case represented by two strangers on their way to a masked ball.

MISTRESS
We'll toast Antonio then . . .

LADY VISITOR
If the champagne is well chilled, I have no objection.

MISTRESS
It's chilled.

MASTER
To . . . Antonio.

DAUGHTER
To the first and only love of my life.

LADY VISITOR
Prophesies never come true, but it's the intention that counts.

MISTRESS
To your health.

MASTER
(After drinking) Yes, to our health . . . Even though at this point that word has about as much real meaning for me as El Dorado or Atlantis.

LADY VISITOR
Or Antonio.

MISTRESS
What are you talking about?

MASTER
I've wanted to tell you for some time now, but I haven't had the courage. You'll have to excuse me, because I'm going to ruin your evening, but I think the presence of these two

new . . . friends will help my wife and daughter to bear up. *(Overplaying the lines like a bad actor, he gets up and starts walking with a limp in the left leg.)* I have only a few months to live. I'm suffering from a rare disease, and the doctor has told me there's no hope.

MISTRESS
(She does not know how to react. Inside, she is pleased, because this way she can run off with the love of her life.) It's not . . . possible. When did you see the doctor? You've hardly been out of the house . . .

MASTER
You were sleeping. You didn't know a thing about it. *(To the Daughter)* And you had left for those open spaces of yours.

DAUGHTER
But couldn't the doctor be wrong? Have you consulted another one?

MASTER
I've seen several. They ran all the tests again, and there's definitely no doubt about it. I am a condemned man.

LADY VISITOR
(With false piety) But you won't be alone. Your wife and your daughter will stay with you up until the very end.

MISTRESS
Is that . . . what you expect from us?

MASTER
Yes, and please *(He kneels before the Mistress and Daughter, who stand at his sides.),* on my knees, I beg of you both, do not leave me alone for a moment. Swear it to me, before these two witnesses from God.

DAUGHTER
No! I can't swear it to you . . . I'm sorry, but . . .

MASTER
(Unconvincingly, like a bad actor, he gets up and starts

limping heavily, this time on the right leg.) But why? . . .

LADY VISITOR
(In the Master's ear, whispering) You're limping on the wrong leg.

DAUGHTER
My dear foster father *(Stroking his cheek with great tenderness),* you're contradicting yourself. Try to remember how one day you told me that when you love someone, they cross over and come to live inside you, because that's what love is, not being afraid of the other, feeling them as part of yourself, reconstructing them inside you. And that's why you will never die within me. You will go on living. I will remember you, and I will keep you healthy and vigorous inside me, so long as I live.

MASTER
(Half irritated, half disoriented) I told you that?

DAUGHTER
Yes . . . and I swear to you that I shall live. I'm brimming with life, intoxicated with it, and from this night on, I swear to burst each bubble of time in mad joy.

MISTRESS
Mad joy . . .

DAUGHTER
Because . . . why should I hide it from you any longer? He has come for me, and I'm not afraid of anyone any more. *(Points to the Lady Visitor)* Not even of this woman who is trying to take him away from me . . . because Antonio is here . . . and he loves me . . . *(She flings herself into the Visitor's arms.)* as much as I love him! *(The Visitor does not embrace her.)* Isn't it true? *(She sees that he does not react favorably, frightened as he is by the presence of the Lady Visitor.)* Didn't you tell me that this very night we were going away together? The two of us, mounted on my horse, wrapped in each other's arms . . .

MISTRESS

My child . . . *(She takes her into her arms when the Daughter lets go of the Visitor, who has remained hieratically still.)* You are confused. And we are all to blame, we grown-ups. We thought it might be too strong an emotion for you, that it might produce too strong a jolt, to let you know . . . that your real parents are alive . . . They are, dear child, our visitors.

DAUGHTER

(Her mental balance greatly shaken) What?

MISTRESS

He is your real father, and she your mother. But today you received the terrible news of your fiancé's breaking your engagement, so it's only natural that your mind is a little disturbed, and . . . yes, you confused your father's effusiveness with something else . . .

DAUGHTER

What do you know about what happened with my fiancé? What broken engagement? *(The Masters of the house exchange looks. The Daughter points at the Visitor.)* He is Antonio! And he has come back to take me away with him.

LADY VISITOR

My daughter . . . we are your parents. Forgive us, but all these years, I promise you, it was we, your father and I, who suffered most from not being with you. But the fact is, we are . . . two outlaws. Ours is a life of crime, and tonight we came here because the police are closing in on us. We are two burglars, and, if you don't believe us, the jewels from our last robbery are hidden in that sofa.

DAUGHTER

(Feeling ill, nauseated, she leans on the Mistress.) No. I don't know, madam, what you are talking about . . .

LADY VISITOR

(Wickedly) Don't call me that . . . *(Suddenly sincere, breaking up inside)* Call me . . . by some other name . . .

(The Visitor has remained motionless, standing in the shadows.)

MASTER
(Feeling emotion) Call her . . . by some other name.

DAUGHTER
(Very upset) Some other name?

MASTER
Yes, let your own blood dictate the word to you.

DAUGHTER
Blood? . . . Still more blood? . . . I saw my own blood flow this afternoon . . .

MASTER
That's all in your imagination.

LADY VISITOR
(To Master, Mistress, and Visitor) Please, leave me alone for a few minutes . . . with my daughter . . .

DAUGHTER
No . . . don't go away . . .

MISTRESS
(Giving her a kiss on the forehead and exiting stage left) Only for a moment . . .

MASTER
We'll be right here, just a few feet away. *(Also kisses her on the forehead and exits. The Visitor looks at her, and the Daughter looks back imploringly. He lowers his eyes and exits.)*

LADY VISITOR
(Very sincere, boldly) You had formed a very different picture . . . of your mother? *(Takes her hand, kisses her, and leads her toward a chair)* Please, sit down, completely calm, just for a moment, that's all . . . *(The Daughter is so lost in the whirlpool of her thoughts that she lets herself be*

led to the chair and seats herself. The Lady Visitor immediately kneels next to her, without letting go of her hand.) On the other hand, I had pictured you exactly like this—an angel. *(She raises the daughter's hand to her cheek.)* I know it's going to be very hard for you, in these circumstances, to grow fond of me. *(The Daughter continues not to respond, pausing.)* In any situation, people have a hard time growing fond of me. *(She is filled with emotion, her voice becomes veiled.)* But in your case, perhaps, it would have been different . . . Having you ever since you were little, day after day . . . perhaps you really might have grown fond of me. I would have been your mama, the one who protected you from everything in the world . . . *(Her voice breaks with sobbing.)* And that way, maybe, you wouldn't have been bothered by . . . my power. How I envied that man, dying or not, when you told him you loved him, and that he'd live on forever within you! *(Crying)* What a relief it would be to know that I am going to go on living, within another soul, fresh and pure as yours! Are you certain . . . that it would be impossible for you to love me? *(Stepping silently, slowly, the Visitor re-enters.)* The man *(The Lady Visitor returns to being her brittle self.)* who came to be your father never loved me. *(Becomes sincere again)* And I am weary of this—my destiny. I don't want to be me any longer . . . Can't you understand that? You are so sensitive. Yes, you are beginning to understand me. And . . . do you know? When you said that to love was to carry someone inside you, I thought that the day I die I might change myself into you . . . you, whom everybody cares for, whom nobody fears . . .

DAUGHTER
But you don't have to die. You're still young, and beautiful. My life with Antonio can't begin this way, with a death. My life with Antonio must be a model of perfection. We two will teach the world to be happy . . .

LADY VISITOR
His name is not Antonio. He is your father.

DAUGHTER
You're trying to mix me up. *(She withdraws her hand from*

41

the Lady Visitor's.) You are not my mother.

VISITOR
She is, and you must respect her, and obey her.

DAUGHTER
(Standing up and taking him by the arms) Why do you say
that? Why are you so afraid of her?

LADY VISITOR
There's no more time to lose. We have to get out of here.
The police have lost our trail, and now we should get on
with our plan.

VISITOR
We'll take her hostage.

DAUGHTER
No! You and I are the ones who have to run away together.
Not her! *(The Visitor covers her mouth with his hand.)*

LADY VISITOR
Yes. That way we'll be sure they won't call the police.

VISITOR
Give me that cloth so I can tie her hands. *(The Lady Visitor
hands him a long doily from one of the pieces of furniture.)*
That goes here . . .

LADY VISITOR
Quick. *(They tie the Daughter's hands.)* And now her
mouth . . . *(She finds another, similar furniture mat and
hands it to the Visitor.)* Here, take it. *(The Daughter resists
but they subdue her easily.)*

VISITOR
Where's the gun?

LADY VISITOR
In my purse, upstairs, with the rest of my clothes.

VISITOR
Go get it now . . . I'll take care of her . . . *(He throws her onto the sofa where they made love. The Daughter cannot defend herself because her hands are tied behind her back. The Visitor proceeds to search for another doily to bind her ankles.)* You never should have come down without the gun.

LADY VISITOR
It's well hidden. *(She looks upstairs, doesn't hear anything and begins to climb the stairs. When she is almost at the top, the Mistress appears at the head of the stairs, holding the gun, a pistol.)*

MISTRESS
Searching for this?

LADY VISITOR
(To the Visitor) Look . . .

VISITOR
(Standing up, going toward the foot of the stairs) Please, madam, be careful. The gun is loaded.

MISTRESS
(Looking at the Visitor) There's somebody one too many here.

LADY VISITOR
Put down that gun at once . . . lay it on the stairs . . .

MISTRESS
(To the Lady Visitor) Get down . . . out of my way . . .

LADY VISITOR
(To the Visitor) Tell her to obey me.

MISTRESS
(Coming down the staircase, addressing the Visitor with all the pent-up love of twenty years) Please, I beg of you, don't make me wait any longer. Tell her you've come for me, and

nothing else. She's going to understand. There's nothing else for her to do . . . Tell her—I am the strong one now, the gun's in my hand. We'll escape together. My car has a full tank of gas . . . but that must only have been an excuse for you to come after me . . . isn't that so? You couldn't bear another second without seeing me . . .

VISITOR

(Icily) Madam, please. Just put down the gun, there, where she showed you.

MISTRESS

I'll kill her if it's necessary. You've no more reason to be afraid of her. Let's go now.

VISITOR

Put down the gun, there. It's loaded. *(Firmly)* And I ask you, please, stop confusing me with someone I'm not. *(The Mistress fires a shot and the Visitor falls dead.)*

LADY VISITOR

What have you done? *(She goes to the Visitor, kneels, and takes him in her arms.)* It's not possible . . . he's dead . . .

MASTER

(Appears at the top of the stairs and addresses the Mistress) Don't be afraid of anything. I'm right here beside you. *(To the Lady Visitor)* And you, don't you be afraid either. I was your husband's best friend, and I'll go on protecting you every way I can.

LADY VISITOR

Protecting me? I despise you thoroughly. I've only known you for a few hours, and that's more than enough for me . . .

MISTRESS

You always were jealous of me, and with very good reason, as now you can see.

LADY VISITOR

You are a lunatic. Now, the only thing to do is load the

corpse into the car. I'll take care of everything else. There's nothing left for you but to cooperate with me. Most of all, don't say a word to the police, because now you, madam, are just as much a criminal as I. We're on the same level. You'll have to cooperate whether you want to or not. The only important thing now is for neither of you to tell the police anything.

MISTRESS
His body belongs to me.

LADY VISITOR
(To the Master) There's no time to lose. That woman is insane. She's never seen this man before in her life. Take the gun away from her, now.

MISTRESS
Enough lies! *(Fires at the Lady Visitor, who falls dead)*

MASTER
(Walks slowly down to where the Lady Visitor lies) A body, right here, stretched out in the middle of the room, blocks the path.

DAUGHTER
(Making what sounds she can, bound and gagged as she is) M-m-m-m-m.

MASTER
Child . . . *(Runs to her)* What you must have gone through! You, fragile as a flower, and in the middle of this witches' sabbath.

MISTRESS
(She has remained motionless, on the same step, midway down the flight of stairs.) I have killed him.

MASTER
Correction. You have killed *them.*

DAUGHTER
(Freed from the gag while the Master goes about untying

her hands and feet) What madness . . . *(Deeply crushed)*
Antonio hadn't done anything to you. Now life has no
meaning for me.

MISTRESS
*(Comes down the stairs slowly; places the pistol next to the
Master and addresses him)* You were right . . . this girl is
deeply disturbed.

MASTER
Now's not the time for splitting hairs. *(To the Daughter)*
Help me get these two stumbling-blocks out of here. *(Grabs
the Lady Visitor by the ankles)* Take hold of her hands.

DAUGHTER
My life has no meaning anymore.

MASTER
Help me, will you! *(The Daughter obeys him.)*

MISTRESS
Don't let my robe drag. It's a souvenir from a trip. *(Master
and Daughter remove the Lady Visitor's body, carrying her
so as not to drag the robe. They exit stage left. The Mistress
approaches the Visitor's corpse, kneels beside him, raises
his head, and kisses his lips.)* But to my life . . . you did
give meaning . . . *(Annihilated within)* and this is how I
repay you . . .

MASTER
(Re-enters with the Daughter) For the time being they can
stay in the pantry. Later they'll go to feed the furnace.

DAUGHTER
(Pouncing on the gun) And me with them . . .

MISTRESS
(Shouts) No!

MASTER
(Quickly prevents the Daughter from raising the gun to her

46

breast) Your life has hardly begun. *(Takes the bullets out of the gun and puts them in his pocket)* What do you know about meaning? *(To the Mistress)* Let's see, help me get him out of here. I don't like having my best friend sprawled out on the floor this way. *(The Mistress grasps the Visitor's hands and the Master his feet. They can't lift him.)*

DAUGHTER
It's useless. He was a giant.

MISTRESS
With muscles like granite.

MASTER
Nonsense. It's his conscience that weighs so heavily. *(The Master pulls the rug on which the corpse is lying and succeeds in taking it out stage left, just like the Lady Visitor's.)*

DAUGHTER
(Begins to smooth her clothes, to fix her hair, still in a trance of deep confusion) But now . . . we're three killers . . . *(The Master and Mistress re-enter.)* We're accomplices to a crime.

MASTER
No, my pet. The two of us are innocent. *(Points to the Mistress)* She's the only guilty party: first an adulterous wife and now a murderess . . .

MISTRESS
No. The three of us, we did it together, by mutual consent, and in self-defense . . .

MASTER
Let's hear none of that. You pulled the trigger all by yourself. I only loaded the revolver and left it within your reach . . .

MISTRESS
It's a plot . . .

MASTER

Hadn't you caught on yet? Ah, but how well everything has
turned out. The unfaithful wife who eliminates her lover,
and, with a single bullet—or, should I say two?—steps out
of the way, leaving her husband to start his life all over . . .
(Addresses the Daughter) Because life has more than one
meaning . . . and I take it upon myself to teach you that.
(Takes hold of her by the arms) I'm not your father, and I
won't be master of this house either. I'll simply be a man
you love . . .

DAUGHTER

Yes, I already love you, with all my heart and soul, but in
another way . . .

MASTER

I'll teach you to love me in a thousand ways.

DAUGHTER

She killed Antonio.

MASTER

She killed your parents

DAUGHTER

Please, I can't stand it any more. Take me away from here.

MASTER

(Embraces her and quickly kisses her on the lips) I knew
you'd understand. Let's get going. *(To the Mistress)* And
you, get busy so nobody discovers what happened this afternoon. You know, everything into the furnace . . . And afterwards, silence. I'll move the convertible away from the
house.

DAUGHTER

Let's leave in it . . . but, please, as fast as possible. I'm
afraid that something even worse is going to happen tonight.

MASTER

All right, . . . my dear. And once in the city, we'll get rid of the car . . . Let's go now.

MISTRESS
No. Please. Don't leave me here alone . . . *(The doorbell rings.)*

MASTER
That must be the maid.

DAUGHTER
Don't open the door.

MASTER
No, that way she might suspect something.

MISTRESS
(To the Master) You open it, please. *(The Master opens the front door and the Doctor and Nurse, in their appropriate professional outfits, appear. They are played by the same actors who played the Visitors, but he no longer wears a beard or mustache.)*

DOCTOR
Good evening.

MASTER
What can I do for you?

DOCTOR
Are you the man of the house?

MASTER
(After a moment's hesitation, he answers with difficulty.)
Yes . . .

MISTRESS
(From where she stands, without moving) And I am his wife. Won't you please come in?

DOCTOR
(Enters with the nurse) Thank you.

MASTER

(Gaining more confidence, he takes a step toward the Doctor and Nurse.) And this is our adopted daughter.

DOCTOR

Very well, then. This morning the Municipal Psychiatric Hospital received a typical call from a family in an emergency situation. The call for help was cut off, but in such cases we systematically trace the call through the operator.

MASTER

It was a foolish thing, actually . . . We were worried about . . . the disappearance *(Points to the Daughter)* of our daughter.

NURSE

(Hastily approaches the Daughter) The young lady needs help?

DAUGHTER

No . . . actually, I was leaving the house, with him. In order to begin a new life, as he put it. No. He said, "Free to start our lives all over again." *(Taking the Master's arm)* Please, tell them, so they stop looking at me that way.

MISTRESS

But, silly, what's this about wanting to go away from here? And your father, why do you want to take him away from his home, where he has all his papers? Remember: he's writing his memoirs . . .

NURSE

(Seeing that the Daughter drops the Master's arm, she approaches the Daughter and takes her by the arm.) You really do need help, don't you?

MASTER

If you want their help, just ask. Would you rather we left you alone with these people?

DAUGHTER

(Looks at the Master) That depends on you. Tell me now:

what do I have to do?

MASTER

Talk with them, if that seems right to you. We grown-ups might be in your way. *(To the Mistress)* Better to leave them alone, don't you think?

DAUGHTER

(Leaves no time for the Mistress to respond) But only with the doctor . . . no one else.

NURSE

(Barely masks her annoyance) I can leave, of course.

MASTER

(Points to the exit, stage left) Let's go this way, then.

MISTRESS

(Remembering that they will find the two bodies that way) No, dear. Not that way. Everything's in a mess out there. *(Points upstairs)* Let's go up to your study.

MASTER

You're right. *(To the Nurse)* This way . . .

NURSE

Thank you. *(Half way up the stairs with the Master and the Mistress, she speaks to the Doctor.)* But don't forget, Doctor, we still have other calls to make, before midnight.

DOCTOR

OK. I'll keep it in mind. *(The Nurse, Master, and Mistress exit at the top of the stairs. The Doctor speaks to the Daughter affectionately and protectively.)* There's something in this house that upsets you, isn't there?

DAUGHTER

No, not anymore. You're what upsets me now. To me, you look very much like a certain . . . Antonio, whom I loved very much.

51

DOCTOR
Why did you stop loving him?

DAUGHTER
Because he died. My foster mother killed him, just a little while ago.

DOCTOR
(Incredulous) Her? Are you sure?

DAUGHTER
If I weren't sure, I would have thrown myself into your arms the minute you walked in, thinking you were him—Antonio. You're just like him. You're very easy to love.

DOCTOR
Think so?

DAUGHTER
Yes. I'm absolutely certain.

DOCTOR
But I'm the doctor.

DAUGHTER
Doesn't matter who you are, it matters *how* you are.

DOCTOR
How am I then?

DAUGHTER
(Closes her eyes) Let me close my eyes. First I have to look at all the dark landscapes inside me.

DOCTOR
Why?

DAUGHTER
Because in the dark, I'll get up the nerve to touch him . . . to touch you. *(She strokes his arm.)* It's very dark in the library of that big old house.

DOCTOR
You're all alone in the library?

DAUGHTER
No. Ever since I came in, I could hear breathing. *(She begins to unbutton the Doctor's shirt.)* I know all your knots and buttonholes very well.

DOCTOR
(Lets her go on, caught up in the eroticism of the situation and, at the same time, pursuing his professional investigation.) But me, how am I? Isn't there a risk that you're taking me for someone else? Someone much better?

DAUGHTER
You are just the way I had always pictured you.

DOCTOR
That's just what I was afraid of. People are always imagining me better than I really am.

NURSE
(Appears at the top to the staircase) Doctor, that's what I was afraid of: that we would get delayed . . . *(She comes downstairs.)*

DOCTOR
(Separates himself from the Daughter, buttoning his shirt) You're right.

NURSE
The masters of the house would rather that we take the young lady with us.

DAUGHTER
I'm obedient. I'll do whatever they say.

NURSE
But you'll be under my custody. The Doctor will only see you for a moment or two in the morning, and once again in the afternoon.

DAUGHTER
(Content, within the limits of her weariness) That's enough for me.

NURSE
(Shows her a white package she came in with and deposited on a piece of furniture) It'll be better if you put on something to keep you warm.

DAUGHTER
(The Doctor unfolds the strait jacket and affectionately puts it on her as they talk.) Has the temperature dropped that much?

DOCTOR
Yes, the night is cool, outside. *(The Master and Mistress appear at the top of the stairs and watch the scene in deep suffering.)*

DAUGHTER
We can leave whenever you want. I'm ready.

MISTRESS
Good-bye, . . . Daughter.

DAUGHTER
Good-bye.

MASTER
Good-bye, my child.

DAUGHTER
Good-bye. *(The Doctor and Nurse nod farewell and exit through the main door, following the Daughter.)*

MASTER
(Comes down the stairs) That's what I was afraid of . . . that one day they'd take her away like this.

MISTRESS
(Very sad) Poor thing.

54

MASTER
(Collapsing within) What a day!

MISTRESS
The joy she brought us was too great. We couldn't bear it, and on our own we began imagining difficulties. From that point to their coming about was a short step.

MASTER
(Drops into one of the chairs, leaning his head onto the arm) Tonight our old age begins. Can't you feel it?

MISTRESS
Yes, but I couldn't have put it in such precise terms.

MASTER
Our two best friends are shot, dead. We didn't know how to understand them. And our daughter is on her way to a ward for the distraught.

MISTRESS
At least our old age may be . . . short.

MASTER
Every minute will be a torment.

MISTRESS
May Heaven take pity on us . . . and finish this quickly.

MASTER
Our old age *could* be . . . short.

MISTRESS
You'd take care of it yourself?

MASTER
Yes. You only have to ask me . . .

MISTRESS
I don't have the courage . . . but you have enough for both of us, don't you?

MASTER
I will be the executor, but you tell me how, when . . .

MISTRESS
(Interrupting) Now . . .

MASTER
But tell me how . . . *(He puts the gun to her temple and the doorbell rings.)*

MISTRESS
Who could that be? Don't open the door!

MASTER
Maybe it's that . . . clown, that quack again. Better open the door and get rid of him fast.

MISTRESS
(Goes to the door, coquettish again, fixing her hair) In that case, I'll go . . . *(She opens the door and in the shadow there stands a girl, modestly dressed in gray clothes that might be confused with a maid's uniform. The character is played by the same actress who played the Daughter.)* What can I do for you?

MAID
(Very animated but extremely humble, almost servile) I'm the person who's going to do things for you, madam.

MASTER
The maid!

MAID
(Enters and curtsies) The one and only!

MISTRESS
(Half satisfied, half disoriented) But at this hour . . .

MAID
I beg your pardon, a thousand times, but I got lost . . . For hours and hours, I've been circling around in these fields.

(Looks around the room, ecstatic) What an inviting place!

MISTRESS
It's a little messy.

MASTER
Yes. There are some rooms you can't even go into, until morning.

MISTRESS
Yes, and the truth is . . . maybe we don't need your services anymore.

MAID
Oh! . . . What a pity that would be, . . . because I was hardly in the door before I felt something special about this house.

MASTER
(Ill at ease) For example . . .?

MAID
I felt that this was . . . a real home.

MISTRESS
Why?

MAID
Well, . . . I'm not the best person to explain that. I never had a home. I'm an orphan. But I'd always pictured a home exactly his way.

MASTER
What way?

MAID
This way, with the gentleman of the house very intelligent, a writer maybe, . . . and the lady very elegant, who leaves her mark on everything she touches. This flower arrangement, for instance.

MISTRESS
(Flattered) But this is an out-of-the-way place, not for young people.

MAID
That's what I like about it—it's so peaceful. And when I want to hear other voices, I can always turn on the radio.

MASTER
You like music?

MAID
Crazy about it. Not so much the serials though, except for one, at ten o'clock. I never miss that.

MISTRESS
Well, we missed it last night.

MAID
I heard it!

MISTRESS
I can't believe it!

MAID
Yes, and I can tell you the story, if you want me to . . .

MASTER
It's 9:30. We could have a bite to eat while you tell us.

MISTRESS
And at 10, we can hear today's episode.

MAID
I can stay then?

MISTRESS
(To the Master) What do you think?

MASTER
She could . . . stay, don't you think so?

58

MISTRESS
I think so too . . . *(To the Maid)* Stay!

MAID
(Deeply moved) Madam *(Sighs in relief)*, what a relief! I
thought all this *(Indicating the house)* was only a dream,
and that all of a sudden I'd wake up, all alone again, in the
darkness of the countryside.

MISTRESS
Well, if it makes you happy, . . . stay . . .

MAID
(Kisses the Mistress' hand, then the Master's) Thank you
. . . thank you! And now I'm going to straighten up all this.

MISTRESS
All right. *(The Maid sets about putting things in order. First
she puts the doilies in their proper places, as if well ac-
quainted with them, and then begins to fluff the cushions.)*
In the meantime, I'll fix a little refreshment.

MASTER
(Moves to extreme stage left, down to the footlights) Listen
(Starts to smile), you've caught on, haven't you?

MISTRESS
*(Feigning, watching over her shoulder, to make sure that
the Maid can not hear them as she arranges the room)* No.
Caught on to what?

MASTER
It's her . . . It's another one of her pranks . . .

MISTRESS
Whose?

MASTER
Our child. She's come back. We haven't lost her.

MISTRESS
(Remote) Do you think so?

MASTER
Yes, I'm sure.

MISTRESS
What makes you say so?

MASTER
Simply . . . because our luck couldn't have been that bad.
She didn't lose her mind, they didn't take her away to the
psychiatric pavilion. She's here, playing with us, just the
way she did when she was a little girl.

MISTRESS
It's true. We never deserved such bad luck.

MASTER
And everything else was pure fear, pure imagination.
There, in that room, there are no two corpses, shot to death,
on the floor. You didn't kill anyone.

MISTRESS
Of course I didn't kill anyone . . . Me? A murderess? Me?
Who all my life have been a peaceful housewife and music
lover?

MASTER
A housewife, with a deep secret, always waiting for the
miracle to repeat itself.

MISTRESS
(Half surprised, half pleased) You knew all along . . .
(Snuggles in his arms, looking up)

MASTER
Yes . . .

MISTRESS
I never stopped waiting for him. I never believed he could
have died that way, so stupidly, in an automobile accident,
back in 1929.

MASTER
And now . . . you're still waiting for him?

MISTRESS
Yes . . .

MASTER
And I'm not going to leave you alone for a second. The minute I see him arrive, I'll fight, right up to the end, for what I love most. I'll defend myself somehow . . . I'll kill him if necessary. *(At this point, the Maid discovers the bag of jewels under the cushion. She opens it and begins to examine the contents, dazzled. The Master and Mistress, lost in their joy, are not aware of her.)*

MISTRESS
None of that, now. Everything will be arranged in a quite gentlemanly manner.

MASTER
You think so?

MISTRESS
Yes, . . . you let yourself get carried away by your imagination. Today we've already killed two people in our delirium.

MAID
There's something hidden here, a bag of jewels.

MASTER
(Amused at the prospect of the game, but not looking at the Maid) Aha! . . . You don't say so? Isn't that fun?

MAID
But, sir, . . . they look real.

MISTRESS
In this house everything is legitimate, starting with our desires.

MAID
But, madam . . .

MASTER
Just like before . . . *(The Maid, frightened by the eccentricities of her employers, tiptoes to the door. Then she looks back and sees the bag of jewels again. Suddenly she feels tempted to go back and get it. She does so, hiding it among the pleats of her uniform. She approaches the door stealthily and finally escapes.)*

MASTER
(To the Mistress with his back turned to the Maid) As you can see . . . there are no dead bodies in the pantry, and our girl has come back. At this very moment, she is not terrified in her dungeon. She's with her parents, who adore her.

MISTRESS
But such waiting, so many anxieties.

MASTER
And if you had to do it all over again, just in order to achieve this moment of peace? If that were the price of this peace?

MISTRESS
This isn't a moment of peace. It's a moment of renewed hope, for his return.

MASTER
I'll fight for what's mine.

MISTRESS
(Flirtatious) I thought I didn't interest you any longer . . .

MASTER
If he comes back for you, that means you're valuable, that you're worth a lot.

MISTRESS
A moment ago, I thought I wanted to die, but it wasn't true.

Only weariness, and now that's passed. And, yes, I'd do it all over again. Everything—endless waiting, horrible anxieties—everything, just so I feel that joy again, one more time.

MASTER
Don't talk so loud, the child might hear you.

MISTRESS
(In hushed tones) That joy. That joy he brought me, those afternoons.

MASTER
(Also in hushed tones) But afterwards? Afternoons are short, they end quickly.

MISTRESS
Afterwards comes the night, and I shut my eyes in peace, under a mantle of stars. *(A police siren is heard.)*

MASTER
A police siren! And it's heading this way . . .

MISTRESS
No! It's going farther out. Don't panic. God only knows where it's headed . . . *(They both listen.)*

MASTER
No, they're coming here. *(The siren sounds nearer.)* And they're looking for us.

MISTRESS
Nonsense. It couldn't be. Not now, when you desire me the way you once did.

MASTER
You're right. *(Car doors are heard slamming.)*

MISTRESS
No. It couldn't possibly be. Don't open the door!

MASTER
No! *(Embraces her tightly)* I promise you. This time I won't. *(The doorbell rings loudly.)*

MASTER
It's the door.

VOICE OF POLICEMAN
Surround the place, nobody gets out alive.

MISTRESS
(Seeing the Master about to open the door) Don't! *(He opens it.)*

POLICEMAN
(The same actor who played the Visitor, now wearing a police uniform) Sir, madam . . . good evening.

MASTER
(Pretending to be calm) Good evening.

MISTRESS
(Terrified) Good evening.

POLICEMAN
My pals and I were worried about you. Everything pointed to this house being invaded by two dangerous criminals.

MISTRESS
(Admiring the Policeman's manner) That's so, but I eliminated them.

MASTER
They're in the pantry, dead.

POLICEMAN
What an extraordinary feat!

MASTER
Executed by my wife. She is a very brave woman.

POLICEMAN
As nimble-fingered as she's elegant, if I may say so.

MASTER
As nimble-fingered as she is elegant . . . and watched over by her husband, who happens to be me.

MISTRESS
What a good feeling, knowing you're protected by law and order, symbolized by you.

POLICEMAN
(*Flattered*) Me? A symbol of order?

MISTRESS
Of order, and of something more. If it weren't for that uniform, I could easily take you for someone else . . . someone I loved a lot.

MASTER
But, dear . . . this man is an agent of the police . . .

MISTRESS
It doesn't matter who he is, it matters how he is.

POLICEMAN
(*Fascinated*) And just how am I? I always wanted to know.

MISTRESS
(*Romantically*) You are . . . exactly the way I imagined you.

CURTAIN

Under a Mantle of Stars had its premier at the Ipanema Theatre in Rio de Janeiro on 20 August 1982, under the direction of Ivan de Albuquerque, with the following cast:

Master of the House	Rubens Corrêa
Mistress of the House	Vanda Lacerda
Daughter	Maria Padilha
Lady Visitor	Leyla Ribeiro
Visitor	Edson Celulari